FAST!

randomhouse.com/kids

ISBN 978-0-7364-3017-3 (trade)
ISBN 978-0-7364-8118-2 (lib. bdg.)

Printed in the United States of America
10 9 8 7 6 5 4 3 2 1

FAST!

Adapted by **BARBARA BAZALDUA**

Illustrated by
CAROLINE LAVELLE EGAN
AND JEAN-PAUL ORPIÑAS

Golden® First Chapters

A GOLDEN BOOK • NEW YORK

CHAPTER 1

I watched as two fighter jets streaked across the sky below me. "What's taking this guy so long?" one of them asked. "Is he really as good as they say he is?"

I flew down through the clouds to join them. They had no idea what was in store. If it was a race they wanted, I'd give it to them!

"Last one to the water tower buys a round of fuel!" one of them challenged.

"I'll give you guys a head start," I replied. "You're gonna need it."

Seconds later, I was shooting past them both. "Eat my dust!" I called.

I had won again!

"Dusty!" cried an old biplane named Leadbottom. "You're daydreamin' again!"

I snapped back to reality. I wasn't thousands of feet in the air, shaking my tail flaps at a couple of jets. I was flying low, spraying Vita-minamulch over a cornfield.

I'm Dusty Crophopper. I live in a quiet little spot called Propwash Junction. I used to spend my days flying straight over a field, turning around, flying back the other way, and turning around again, dusting the crops. It wasn't exactly the most exciting thing a plane could do.

I might have been a crop duster on the outside, but on the inside I was a champion racer. All I needed was the chance to show the world what I could do. My dream? To fly in the Wings Around The Globe Rally!

My boss, Leadbottom, just didn't understand.

"Why would ya want to give up crop-dustin'?" he asked as he dropped a huge

3

cloud of stinky Vita-minamulch on the field below. He was a plane who loved his work!

But I wasn't letting Leadbottom get me down. A race to get a spot in the Wings Around The Globe Rally was coming up soon. I was determined to try out.

My best pal, Chug, a fuel truck, was helping me get ready. As soon as I was done spraying for the day, I radioed him. He drove out to the edge of the airfield and coached me over the radio. "Come on, buddy. Keep it going!" he called as I bobbed and weaved over the cornfields.

Everything was going great until I started to leak oil. Dottie was not going to be happy. She was Propwash Junction's trusty mechanic. I'd been going to her for a lot of repairs lately.

"You've worn out your main bearing oil seal," Dottie said after checking under my hood. She looked at me suspiciously and asked if I'd been racing again.

"*Noooo,*" I answered as innocently as possible.

Just then, Chug roared into the repair shop. "Oh, man, Duster, you were in the zone!" he burst out. "Where a Saturn rocket couldn't catch ya! We're talking light speed!"

I gave him a look that I hoped would get him to stop talking, but it was too late. Dottie frowned.

"Dusty, you're not built to race," she told me. "You're built to dust crops. Do you know what will happen if you push it too far?"

Sure, I knew all the awful things that *could* happen: wing flutter, metal fatigue, turbine failure. . . . Dottie had told me that any one of them could ground me for good.

But I also knew what would happen if I didn't try. I'd spend the rest of my airborne days wondering if I could have done something sky-high stupendous—and wishing I had at least tried.

I was going to fly in that qualifying race. And I was going to show them all that I was a racer.

Later that night, as Chug and I watched *The Ten Best Air Crashes of All Time* on the Racing Sports Network, Chug started to worry about what could go wrong in the race.

"Maybe we need some help," he said. That was when he suggested we talk to Skipper, an old Corsair plane who lived in a hangar at the end of the runway. Skipper was rumored to have been a famous flight instructor in the navy.

I had my doubts about going to Skipper. Nowadays he was a grumpy old crankshaft who didn't even fly anymore.

But Chug insisted, so we got up our courage and taxied over. "I heard stories about his squadron, the Jolly Wrenches," Chug whispered. "They were the roughest, toughest, meanest fliers in the navy."

Chug's words weren't exactly making me feel confident. Still, I took a deep breath, rang the hangar bell, and waited.

At last the door opened, and Skipper scowled down at me. Sparky, the tug who pushed him everywhere, waited nearby.

"Hey there, Skipper! I was wondering if you would . . . train me?" I stammered.

Skipper gave me a look that would blister the paint off your wings and slammed the door. So much for help from the legendary flight instructor. I was on my own.

CHAPTER 2

As I headed to the qualifying race in Lincoln, Nebraska, I had a bubbly feeling in my fuel tank. You know, the way you feel when you're excited about something, but nervous, too. I was awfully glad to have Chug and Dottie along to help me.

Soon after we arrived at the airstrip, a sleek racer thundered overhead. Two smaller racers flew next to him. I couldn't believe it! It was *Ripslinger*! He'd won the rally three times. In fact, he was so good, he was prequalified. The two planes flying with him were Ned and Zed, the Twin Turbos. These guys were world-class racers!

I joined the other competitors at the

race official pitty's stand and listened to the instructions.

"Today's qualifying round is one lap around the pylons," the official announced. "The top five finishers will qualify for the Wings Around The Globe Rally."

A plane named Fonzarelli went first and blasted through the course. While Chug fueled me up and Dottie gave my wings a quick once-over, I watched racer after racer take the lap. At last I heard the official call the name I was using for the race: "Strut Jetstream." This was it!

Fonzarelli was in fifth place. I had to beat his time if I wanted a shot at flying in the rally.

"You gotta be kidding me," sneered Ripslinger. "That farmer's gonna *race*?"

Then he and his pals—and soon the entire crowd—laughed as I rolled down the tarmac. I tried to block them out and just focus.

I revved my engines and took off, flying low. The crowd stopped laughing as I roared toward the pylons. I barreled through the zigzag course and zoomed across the finish line.

Chug and Dottie rushed over to congratulate me. "Way to go, Dustmeister!" Chug cried.

I felt great! I had done my best and made it smoothly through the lap.

But my best wasn't good enough. I had come in a tenth of a second behind Fonzarelli. I wasn't going to the rally.

Fonzarelli rolled up. "Hey, pal. Sixth place ain't nothin' to be ashamed of," he said. "That was a heck of a run."

"Thanks," I said. I knew he was trying to make me feel better.

When I got back to Propwash Junction, I packed up all my racing stuff and put it away. It was time to face facts: I was a crop duster, not a racer.

CHAPTER 3

A couple of days later, a delivery truck bounced down the dirt road and skidded to a stop in front of Chug's fueling station, the Fill 'n' Fly. The race official pitty rolled out of the delivery truck, seeming a little rattled from the ride.

"I'm looking for Strut Jetstream," he said, checking his clipboard.

Suddenly I was embarrassed by the name. "It's actually pronounced Dusty Crophopper," I said as I rolled up.

Then the pitty dropped a bombshell. Fonzarelli had been disqualified from the rally for cheating. Which meant . . . which meant . . . *I was in the rally!*

"Dusty's in the race!" Chug yelled.

Everybody in town gathered around me.

"You're gonna cross oceans thousands o' miles wide!" said Chug. "Freezin' your rudder off one day—"

"And burnin' it off the next!" Sparky chimed in.

Then they started talking about hurricanes, cyclones, typhoons, and tornadoes. I felt sort of strange. I mean, I wanted this. But now that it was happening, I wondered if I could really *do* it.

Later, I looked at the route of the rally on a map. It stretched across several continents and all kinds of terrain. I started to realize that this could get kind of dangerous.

Then I realized Skipper was in the doorway. "You'll end up a smokin' hole on the side of a mountain with your parts spread over five countries," he said. "You're going up against the best racers in the world, and some of them don't even finish."

He told me all the things I did wrong when I was racing—and then he told me how to fix them.

"Wait, are you giving me pointers?" I asked cautiously.

But Skipper didn't want to train me. He wanted me to drop out of the race.

"I'm just tryin' to prove that maybe I can do more than I was built for," I insisted.

Skipper gave me a good long look—and then made a decision. "Oh five hundred tomorrow," he said. "Don't be late."

Yeah! Skipper was going to coach me! I was feeling better already.

CHAPTER 4

I was up before dawn, revved up and ready to train! Skipper, Chug, and Sparky rolled to their places at the end of the runway while I took off.

"You want speed, right?" Skipper asked over the radio. "Serious, bolt-rattlin' speed?"

"Oh, yeah!" I said.

"Then look up," he ordered. "The Highway in the Sky. With tailwinds like nothin' you've ever flown. What are you waiting for?"

I looked at the long lines of thin white clouds above me. They were like streets high in the sky. Really high. I mean, we are talking serious altitudes.

I shut my eyes, gritted my teeth, and

started to climb. I was doing okay—until I looked down. The ground seemed to spin below me. Feeling sick with panic, I peeled out of the clouds and headed in for a landing.

I was still trying to catch my breath when Skipper rolled over to me.

"What just happened up there?" he demanded.

"I'm, uh, low on fuel," I lied.

But Skipper wasn't buying it. "The Jolly Wrenches have a motto: *Volo Pro Veritas*. It means 'I fly for truth.' Clearly, you don't! Sparky, push me back to the hangar."

"I'm afraid of heights," I muttered quickly. I'd never admitted that to anyone before, not even to Chug.

Skipper looked shocked.

"And you want to race around the world?" he asked in disbelief.

"Ah, Skip?" said Sparky. "During the attack of Tujunga Harbor, why, even P-38s had trouble at high altitudes. Then, after the war, those 38s went on to win races!"

Sparky and Chug argued back and forth about how phenomenal the P-38s were.

"All right!" Skipper finally said. Sparky and Chug had worn him down. "So you're a flat-hatter. We'll work on that, but for now, let's see if we can turn low and sloppy into low and fast."

Skipper had me fly a training course that would improve my skills. Then, when a commuter plane flew overhead, he told me to race its shadow to the water tower. The shadow won easily.

Skipper pushed me to improve my turns and increase my airspeed. I flew the course over and over again, trying to do everything the way he taught me. Days later, I raced the plane's shadow again—and won!

When I landed, Skipper didn't say much, but I could tell from his grin that he was proud of me. He asked Sparky to paint a

Jolly Wrenches logo on me. I felt honored to wear the insignia of Skipper's old squadron. "You've earned it," he said.

I sure wished he could come with me to the rally. "Just radio back when you get to the checkpoints," he told me. "I'll be your wingman from here."

CHAPTER 5

It was nighttime when I approached JFK Airport in New York. The first leg of the rally would start there. I had never seen so many lights. This definitely wasn't Propwash Junction!

"Crophopper Seven, you are supposed to be on the Canarsie visual. Maintain one thousand feet, intercept the twenty-two right localizer. You are cleared for the ILS twenty-two right approach," radioed the air traffic controller.

Huh? I had no idea what he was talking about. I was about to ask him to repeat his instructions when I saw the runway lights and headed toward them. But as soon as

I touched down, a huge jet nearly landed right on top of me! I turned and almost ran into another plane. Tugs rushed past, blasting their horns. No matter which way I turned, someone was coming at me! This was one busy airport!

A tug gave me directions to pit row. That was where all the planes in the rally were supposed to gather. I finally saw a row of hangars with a banner that said WELCOME RACERS.

Wow! I thought. *That means me! I'm really here with amazing, famous racers from all over the world!*

Just then, I saw one of my heroes. It was the British racing champion Bulldog.

I rushed up. "The Big Dog!" I said. "I saw you do this unbelievable high-g vertical turn. How did you do that?"

"Well, let me tell you!" he said. "In fact, why don't I tell you *all* my racing secrets?"

"Really?" I couldn't believe my luck.

"No!" Bulldog snapped. "This is a competition. Every plane for himself. Goodbye." Then he turned his tail on me.

I had only wanted to tell him how much I admired him. Embarrassed, I turned away—and nearly ran straight into a sleek racer from India. I was so nervous, I accidentally knocked over a pile of oil cans! I waited for her to make a snooty comment, but she just asked if I was all right.

"Sure, why wouldn't I be?" I replied. "And you are Pan-Asian champion and Mumbai Cup record holder Ishani!"

"Most people call me just Ishani," she said with a smile.

"I'm Dusty. I mean, my *name* is Dusty. I'm not *actually* dusty. I'm . . . quite clean," I replied, fumbling for words. What was my problem?

"It is very nice to meet you, quite-clean Dusty," Ishani answered politely.

Well, at least she seems nice, I thought as

she rolled away. I sure hoped Ishani and I would talk again sometime.

Then I spotted Ripslinger. He and his team had a fancy setup nearby.

"Hey, look who made it!" Ripslinger called. "It's the crop duster."

Suddenly, a teardrop-shaped plane called a Gee Bee made a dramatic entrance wearing a mask and cape. It was El Chupacabra—also known as El Chu—the indoor racing champion of Mexico! I knew all about him. He was super famous in his country. He sang on bestselling records. He was on TV. He even wrote romance novels! This was his first long-distance rally, too. He seemed really happy to meet me.

"We will have many adventures, you and I," he said. "I will see you in the skies, amigo!"

The next morning, cheering fans crammed the stands for the beginning of the rally.

"This is *the* flagship event of the world's fastest sport, where only the best of the best compete," Brent Mustangburger, the rally announcer, told the crowd. "Each leg brings a new challenge, testing agility, navigation, and endurance."

Cameras flashed and confetti showered down on us as we emerged from a tunnel at one edge of the runway. When Ripslinger rolled onto the tarmac, the crowd began to scream and cheer. Everyone thought he was a sure winner.

I rolled up next to El Chu and took my position. Suddenly, I heard my new pal gasp.

"Who is that vision?" he asked. He was staring at a plane on the other side of the runway.

"That's Rochelle, the Canadian rally champ," I told him.

"She is like an angel sent from heaven, like a sunrise after a lifetime of darkness." El Chu sighed. He was in love!

But there was no time for that now. We would be taking off any minute! This leg would take us across the North Atlantic to Iceland. The first plane to land would get to be the first one to take off the next day.

"Racers, start your engines!" the judge called.

The fans went wild as we all revved up. Then the pitty dropped his flag and I began my takeoff roll. I was actually doing it! I was about to fly in the Wings Around The Globe Rally!

CHAPTER 6

As I rose over the stands, rough winds created by the bigger planes knocked me around some, but I managed to keep going. I saw the other racers pull away from me and soar over the Long Island Sound. They climbed until they looked like little specks in the big blue sky.

I flew low, following the coastline north. The air got colder, hail pelted me, and snow swirled everywhere, so I could barely see where I was going. Suddenly, a huge shape appeared out of nowhere. An iceberg! I banked hard and felt a jolt as my wheels scraped ice.

When I finally touched down in Iceland,

I discovered I had come in dead last.

"You do know this is a *race,* right?" Ripslinger asked.

I just smiled as if everything was fine and kept on going.

I passed El Chu on the way to my hangar. He was trying to get close to Rochelle—but it wasn't going very well. She was so cold to El Chu, she might as well have been one of those icebergs out in the ocean.

My friends at Propwash Junction radioed in to check on me.

"What's it like racing with the big dogs, Duster?" Chug asked.

"Well, my wings froze solid, I had icicles hangin' off my sprayer, and I nearly smashed into a ten-story iceberg," I replied.

"Awesome!" exclaimed Chug. He didn't seem to understand how much trouble I'd been in.

Skipper did, though. "Dusty, just like when the Jolly Wrenches were up in the

Aleutians, the air down close to the sea has more moisture, which is why you took on ice," he said. "You gotta try to fly higher."

Skipper was right, but that was the last thing I wanted to hear!

CHAPTER 7

The next day, we all got ready to leave for the leg to Germany. But this time, we weren't allowed to use any instruments. We had to navigate by sight alone.

I was the last to take off, but I was moving nice and steady. Suddenly, I heard a distress call from Bulldog.

"Mayday, mayday, mayday! I'm blinded!" he said over the radio.

His engine had sprung a leak, and oil was spurting into his eyes.

I knew I had to do something—and fast. I rushed to Bulldog's side as he went into a downward spiral.

"Bulldog!" I called. "Quick, pull up!"

The ground rushed toward us. "Harder! Harder!" I cried. We zoomed under a bridge and headed straight for a castle.

"Pull up, hard roll right!" I shouted.

I guided Bulldog through the castle towers, but we still had a long way to go. Bulldog was worried that I'd abandon him.

"I'm right here," I said. "I'll fly right alongside you."

Bulldog and I followed a river while the other racers landed at the airport. They cleared the runway as we came into view. I helped Bulldog land by telling him exactly what to do and when to do it. The waiting crowd cheered as our tires touched down safely.

When fire trucks hosed the oil off Bulldog, he was surprised to see that I was the one who had helped him.

"*You* saved me?" he exclaimed. "What did I tell you, boy? Every plane for himself!"

"Where I come from, if you see someone falling from the sky—" I began.

"Yes!" Bulldog interrupted. "But this is a competition! Now you're dead last . . . and I owe you my life." He looked like he had tears in his eyes.

Ripslinger came up behind me. "You are a nice guy," he said. "And we all know where nice guys finish." He rolled off, chuckling.

I was glad I had helped Bulldog, but I had to admit, being in twenty-first place didn't feel too great.

A little while later, El Chu and I were sitting at a German oil hall. We were both feeling lower than a flat tire.

"At least you are not last in the race for love," El Chu told me. He was upset because Rochelle still wouldn't have anything to do with him.

Then a tiny car drove over to us. "My name is Franz, and I would like to say *danke* for representing all us little planes," he said.

I was confused. Franz was a car!

He explained that he was one of only six flying cars ever built. Then he clicked a button and—*presto!*— wings swung out from his sides!

Now he was a plane. His name was Von Fliegenhosen. Even his personality changed. He was suddenly a take-charge kind of guy!

Von Fliegenhosen turned back into Franz. Then he suggested that I get rid of my sprayer. He thought I'd be faster without it.

El Chu agreed. "Perhaps you need to start thinking like a racer," he said.

So later that night, I had my crop-dusting pipes and tank removed. I even got a new paint job!

The next morning, I decided to try out the new me with a practice flight. Without the sprayer, I was lighter and faster. I felt more like Dusty the Racer instead of Dusty the Crop Duster.

CHAPTER 8

We were heading to India next. Ripslinger was still in the lead, but by now several racers had dropped out because of equipment failure.

The rules were that we had to fly low and stay under a thousand feet. I liked the sound of that!

I passed racer after racer as I weaved through the mist-wrapped hills. I easily zipped around rocky peaks, and maneuvered through narrow passages.

I didn't know it at the time, but after I helped Bulldog, racing fans around the world had begun to root for me. Knowing that wouldn't have changed anything. I just wanted to fly my best. Sure, I wanted to win the rally. But I also wanted to make Skipper proud.

When I landed, the press surrounded me. I discovered I had moved from last place all the way up to eighth! It was the biggest one-day move in the rally's history.

Ripslinger glared at me. He didn't like me being the center of attention instead of him. At the time, I didn't know I'd made a serious enemy. I was too busy feeling on top of the world!

Meanwhile, the press fired questions at me. "Where did you learn to race?" one reporter asked.

"From my coach, Skipper. He's the reason

I'm even here," I replied. "He's an amazing instructor and a great friend. He flew dozens of missions all around the world. And I'm sure if he could, he'd be with us right now."

Weeks after the race was over, Sparky told me what had happened next. Back in Propwash Junction, Skipper had heard me on the radio. I guess what I said made him want to try to fly again for the first time in years. Sparky took Skipper onto the moonlit runway.

He watched anxiously while Skipper unfolded his wings and revved his engine. His wheels inched forward, and for a moment, Skipper looked as if he might try to fly. But then he gave up, shut down his engine, and refolded his wings.

CHAPTER 9

The next part of our route was going to be a big challenge for me. I'm talking really big. We were flying over the Himalayas, the highest mountains in the world. Just thinking about that kind of altitude made my rudders shake. I called my friends in Propwash Junction for a pep talk.

"The good thing about being that high up, there's not a lot of oxygen, so if you crash, no explosion," Chug pointed out.

Hearing Chug talk about crashing did not calm my nerves.

I asked Skipper about flying *through* the mountains instead of over them.

"Bad idea," he said. "The Wrenches flew

through terrain like that in the Assault of Kunming. Wind comin' over the peaks can stir up rotors that'll drag you right down. You can fly a whole lot higher than you think."

I sure hoped he was right.

The next day's flight was all I could think about, but El Chu had something else on his mind: Rochelle. He was spending every moment on the ground trying to get her attention. Nothing was working.

I was giving him some advice when Ishani appeared. El Chu could see how much I liked her and left us alone. That was when Ishani invited me to go with her to see the world-famous Taj Mahal.

As we flew together, Ishani mentioned the upcoming race over the Himalayas. She had noticed that I liked to fly low, and she had a suggestion for me.

"You could follow the Iron Compass instead—railroad tracks through a valley in the mountains," she advised.

I was grateful for her help.

The next morning after we took off, I broke away from the other racers and found the train tracks. Following them worked for a while. But as the tracks curved between the enormous peaks, the valley got a lot narrower. I had very little room to maneuver. And then, suddenly, I had none. A mountain was directly in front of me. The tracks disappeared into a dark tunnel that went through it.

I climbed higher, trying not to panic.

I would have to fly over the mountains after all. There was no other choice. But the higher I flew, the more terrified I became. I just couldn't do it. I couldn't fly high enough to get over those peaks. So I made a bold choice: I would fly through the tunnel!

I gathered my courage, dipped back down, and zoomed into the darkness. Red-hot sparks shot from the tips of my wings as they scraped the walls of the narrow tunnel. I saw a pinpoint of light in the distance. I was so relieved. It must be the exit!

I had almost reached it when I heard *TOOOOOOOT!* There was a train chugging toward the tunnel from the other direction.

I had to get out of there!

Every bolt strained and creaked as I flew faster and faster. The train's wheels shrieked and its brakes screamed. Then I burst from the tunnel into a cloud of smoke and steam.

After that, everything was peaceful. So peaceful that I wondered if I was still alive.

Then I spotted a runway down in a valley and landed. A local race official rolled over to greet me. "Welcome to Nepal," he said.

"Have the others left already?" I asked, thinking maybe I was last.

"No one else is here yet," he replied.

Risking the tunnel might have taken a few miles off my life, but it had put me miles ahead in the race. I was in first place!

The other racers were amazed when they heard what I'd done, but Ishani seemed to be avoiding me. I noticed she was wearing a new Skyslycer Mark 5 propeller. Those propellers were made exclusively for Ripslinger's race team.

I suddenly realized what Ishani had done. She had given me bad advice so that Riplinger would give her one of his fancy propellers.

When I confronted her, she replied, "I really thought that you'd just turn around."

"Well, you were wrong," I answered. "And I was wrong about *you*."

CHAPTER 10

I felt bad about losing Ishani as a friend. I still had a lot of flying to do, though. I tried not to think about it.

As we headed for China, I zigzagged through rice paddies and soared over the Great Wall of China. Ripslinger and I were battling it out for first place.

When we landed in Shanghai, I was greeted by a cheering crowd. Working vehicles seemed to be my biggest fans. Who knows—maybe seeing a crop duster get so far in the race made them feel hopeful about their own dreams.

"You're really showin' them big-time racers a thing or two!" Skipper said when I radioed him from a hangar at the airport.

The other competitors and I were heading out across the Pacific the next day. We'd be making a quick fuel stop in Hawaii before continuing on to Mexico. I really needed Skipper's advice. He had flown over the Pacific during the war. He would know what to expect.

"Back in 'forty-one, during the Battle of Wake Island, the Wrenches ran into serious monsoons," he said. "Be careful. And one more thing: I'm proud of you, Dusty."

That meant a lot, coming from a legend like Skipper. If he thought I had what it took to be a champion racer, then so did I.

Just then, Dottie and Chug came on the radio. They had a big surprise.

"We're gonna meet you in Mexico!" they exclaimed. Even Skipper was coming. They were all traveling by cargo plane. I was thrilled! It would be great to see my friends.

When I went to tell El Chu the news, he was preparing to sing a love song to

Rochelle. "Tonight I shall win her heart!" he declared.

I followed him to Rochelle's hangar, where he set up a boom box underneath her balcony. He turned it on and a hard, fast beat blasted out. Then he started singing—well, it was more like shouting—to the music.

Rochelle came to see what all the noise was about. "No, no, no!" she yelled. She slammed the balcony doors.

I quickly pulled the plug on the boom box. El Chu needed help—now!

I signaled to a couple of tugs wearing mariachi outfits, who rolled up and began gently shaking maracas. Then I lit some candles to set a romantic mood.

"Low and slow," I told El Chu.

This time, El Chu crooned his song to Rochelle as the tugs sang backup. When she opened her balcony door and looked out again, El Chu bowed to her.

"Buenas noches, querida," he said softly. "Good evening, beloved."

Rochelle smiled. It was clear that my pal's serenade had worked its magic.

El Chu turned to me. "I am in your debt, compadre," he said. "If ever you need me, I shall be there."

CHAPTER 11

The next morning, the rest of the racers and I rolled past the board that showed our positions in the rally. I was in first place, and Ripslinger was in second. I couldn't help grinning as I prepared for takeoff.

"This is our sixth and longest leg," announced Brent Mustangburger. "Racers will need to follow their GPS antennas, because there's a big ocean between here and Mexico."

Once again, the other racers quickly climbed above the clouds, but I stayed low. I was following my GPS through the fog when one of Ripslinger's teammates, Zed, zoomed up from out of nowhere, closed

in—and snapped off my antenna!

"Oh, no!" I cried as I watched it sink beneath the waves.

The other racers were far ahead of me. I couldn't even hear their engines. I was alone in the middle of the Pacific Ocean with no way to tell where I was going. I tried to steer toward the glow of the sun, but the fog was too thick.

"Hawaii, are you there? Do you read? I am low on fuel," I radioed frantically. The radio was silent. No one could hear me.

DING! My fuel light came on. I was in big trouble!

"Unknown rider, unknown rider," a voice boomed. "You have entered restricted airspace."

Bravo, a U.S. Navy fighter jet, appeared beside me. Another jet, Echo, pulled up on the other side.

I had never been so glad to see anyone in my life.

When I explained what had happened, Echo and Bravo told me to follow them to their aircraft carrier, the *Dwight D. Flysenhower.*

I couldn't believe it! That was Skipper's old ship! I wasn't sure I could land on a moving runway, but as Echo pointed out, I didn't have much choice.

Echo and Bravo talked me down toward the boat. Then the crew waved me onto the deck, and I touched down. A net kept me from shooting off into the sea. When I staggered out, everyone cheered.

"Let's get you fixed up, refueled, and back in the race," Bravo said. "You are way behind."

"Thanks, guys," I replied. "You saved my tail out there." We took an elevator down to the hangar deck, where I saw a wall crammed with pictures and medals.

"That's the Jolly Wrenches Wall of Fame," Bravo explained.

"Every flier, every mission!" Echo added.

I quickly found Skipper's picture, but there was only one mission listed for him. That didn't make any sense.

Later that night, I called Skipper from the radio on the aircraft carrier and asked about the Wall of Fame.

"They only list one mission for you," I told him.

"Dusty," said Skipper, "if you're not past that storm yet, you need to—"

"Is it true?" I asked.

"It's true," Skipper admitted reluctantly.

I was shocked, but just then, the chief petty pitty rushed in. The storm was getting worse, and I had to leave right away.

"Get above the storm," a shooter tug told me as he hooked me to a catapult, which is like a giant slingshot.

"Go win it for the Wrenches, Dusty!" Bravo cried. *"Volo Pro Veritas!"*

Seconds later, I was flung into the air. I heard the tugs cheering on the deck below. I was on my own with miles to fly.

All the other racers had already arrived in Mexico, and they were wondering what had happened to me. El Chu told me later that everyone had been worried—except Ripslinger. He thought that getting rid of me was the right thing to do. As far as he was concerned, having a crop duster in the rally was an insult to the sport of racing.

Meanwhile, I was flying as fast as I could, struggling to make up for lost time. But as I flew, I couldn't stop thinking about Skipper. Had he really flown just one mission? Were all the stories about him made up? And if they were, why hadn't he just said so?

Suddenly, thunder rumbled above me, and dark clouds started to gather. A bad storm was coming fast, and I needed to fly above it.

I started to climb, but a thunderclap scared me. I went back down. I just couldn't push past my fear, no matter how much I needed to.

I was flying above the ocean when rain, thunder and lightning, and wind hit me hard. The waves below got higher and higher, until one crashed right over me. My engine coughed, sputtered, and died.

"Mayday! I am going down!" I radioed. As I hit the icy water, I felt my landing gear crack and my wings buckle. The dark sea swallowed me. *So this is how my dream is going to end?* I thought. Suddenly, a net splashed down around me. As it pulled me to the surface, I saw a Mexican navy helicopter hovering overhead. Then everything went black.

CHAPTER 12

I woke up in a hangar in Mexico with my friends gathered around me. I could tell from the looks on their faces that I was in bad shape.

Dottie delivered the news. "Broken wing ribs, twisted gear, bent prop, your main spar is cracked . . . bad," she said. "It's over."

I was too badly damaged to finish the rally. But I had something else on my mind. All the confusion and hurt I had felt since I'd seen the Wall of Fame came spilling out.

"One mission? So much for *Volo Pro Veritas*," I said to Skipper.

Skipper asked the others to leave us alone. Then he told me about when he had been a young flight instructor with a squadron of rookies. "All razor sharp," Skipper said. "I should know—I trained every single one of 'em."

He had led them out on what was supposed to be a routine patrol. But it had turned into a blazing firefight.

No matter how hard he fought to save his students, Skipper watched them go down in flames, one after the other. Then he was hit. When he woke up on the rescue ship, he learned that his whole squadron had been destroyed.

"After that . . . I just couldn't bring myself to fly again," he finished.

As I tried to work through what Skipper had just told me, he asked me something. "If you knew the truth about my past, would you have asked me to train you?"

I didn't know what to say.

"I'm sorry," Skipper said as I turned and rolled away as best I could.

The next morning I told Dottie what had happened. "Can you believe it?" I asked. "He hasn't been straight with me this whole time. At least you were honest. You said I wasn't built for this. I guess I should have listened to you."

"If you had listened to me, I'd never, ever forgive myself," Dottie replied. "Skipper may have been wrong for what he did, but he was right about you. You're not a crop duster. You're a *racer*. And now the whole world knows it."

It was nice of her to say so. I knew she was trying to make me feel better, but it was hopeless. I was too busted up.

"Look at me—"

"Yes! Look at you!" Suddenly, El Chu was in the hangar doorway with a pair of wings from a T33 Shooting Star on a cart.

He moved aside and I saw Rochelle, Bulldog, and the rest of the racers. They

didn't want to compete without me, so they had all brought me new parts to use! Even Ishani was there with her Skyslycer Mark 5 propeller.

"This one didn't really suit me," she said. "But I think you will have a lot better luck with it."

Dottie and the other racers' mechanics went to work. As they hammered and welded me back together, Chug looked at footage showing highlights from previous races. Over and over again, he watched the parts that showed Ripslinger crossing the finish line.

Then he started to grin. He had noticed something that might make a big difference in who crossed the finish line first the next day.

CHAPTER 13

Planes stared as I rolled onto the tarmac for the last leg of the rally. I finally looked like a racer!

"We'll see you in New York!" Dottie yelled.

"It's dustin' time!" called Chug.

Meanwhile, Ripslinger looked angrier than ever. "Bolting on a few new parts doesn't change who you are," he snarled. "I can still smell the farm on you."

Then I realized something. "I finally get it," I said. "You're afraid of getting beat by a crop duster." I rolled up to Ripslinger and looked him in the eye. "Well, check six. 'Cause I'm coming."

For once, Ripslinger couldn't think of anything mean to say.

The final leg was all about speed. I had to start last, but I didn't plan to finish last. I was going to do my best to make sure I was the first racer across the finish line in New York!

I watched my fellow racers—now my friends—take off. Then it was my turn. I zoomed over towns and villages, blazed around the slopes of mountains, and sprinted past the shadows of Bulldog and the other racers. Tenth place . . . eighth . . . sixth. I was catching up!

At last I saw Ripslinger, Ned, and Zed ahead of me as we soared over the desert. I didn't hear Ripslinger tell his teammates that it was time to finish me off. I didn't have to, because I saw them coming for me.

While Ned and Zed hurled insults my way, Ripslinger closed in from above. He pushed me toward the rocks with his landing gear. There was nowhere to go. I was going to crash!

Then, suddenly, Skipper came streaking through the sky! I couldn't believe he was flying! He dived straight at Ripslinger and drove him away from me. That gave me the chance to pull up, but Ned and Zed were instantly on my tail.

I flew sideways into a chasm. When Ned and Zed followed, they slammed into each other and got stuck in the space between the rocks. But then Ripslinger snuck up on Skipper. He tore into Skipper's tail with his propeller.

I raced over, but to my surprise, Skipper was grinning. Ripslinger had damaged his own prop in the attack.

"I'll live," Skipper told me. "Go get him!"

I gave it all I had, but Ripslinger stayed just ahead of me. I poured on the power, but it wasn't enough. Then I noticed shadows rippling over me and looked up. There it was: the Highway in the Sky.

I remembered Skipper's words. *"Tailwinds like nothin' you've ever flown."*

But I had to climb if I wanted to ride them. *I can do this,* I thought. *I have to do this.* I took a deep breath, shut my eyes, and pulled up hard.

"Don't look down, don't look down," I chanted.

The wind whistled past me and the ground fell farther and farther away. I ignored the dizzying waves of fear and kept going.

Then—*WHUMP!* I punched through the clouds and felt the tailwinds catch me. "Whoa! Yeah!" I screamed as I blazed across the sky. I caught up to Ripslinger in no time.

The city was below us now. I only had a few more miles to fly. Ripslinger didn't even see me coming.

In the stands below, fans screamed with excitement as I drew closer and closer.

As we neared the finish line, Ripslinger tilted toward the cameras. He wanted to make sure the press got good pictures of him when he won. Chug had seen this in the footage and told me Rip would do that, so I was ready for it.

I swerved to the other side, passed Ripslinger—and burst through the ribbon! I had won the Wings Around The Globe Rally!

"He's done it! He's done it!" Brent

Mustangburger screamed into the microphone again and again.

Ripslinger was so surprised, he crashed into a line of portable toilets!

My friends gathered around me, cheering wildly. Even Franz was there! And he had brought a crowd of working vehicles with him! "You are an inspiration to all of us," he said. "All of us who want to do more than just what we were built for."

I looked at everyone and realized how grateful I was for their help. I couldn't have done it without them. But there was one friend in particular I wanted to thank. I watched with the rest of the crowd as he soared overhead, then came in for a landing. I went straight over to him.

"Thanks, Skip," I said.

"Don't thank me," he replied. "I learned a lot more from you than you ever learned from me."

EPILOGUE

"**A**ttention on deck!" the landing signal officer shouted. A line of jets saluted as Skipper rolled onto the deck of the *Dwight D. Flysenhower.*

"It's an honor to be here," Skipper said.

It was for me, too. The squadron had made me an honorary Jolly Wrench!

Moments later, Skipper and I were hooked up to the catapults.

"Well, they didn't have these fancy toys the last time I did this," Skipper said.

I told Skipper there was nothing to it. All he had to do was nod to the shooter tug and hold on tight.

"*Yeeeaahh!*" we shouted as we were

launched into the air.

My friend Skipper was back in the sky—
and I was right there beside him.

I couldn't wait to see where our adventures
took us next!